About the Author

Jennifer Brozek is a multi-talented author, editor, and tie-in writer who has been nominated and won professional awards. She is the author of *Never Let Me Sleep*, and *The Last Days of Salton Academy*, both of which were nominated for Bram Stoker Award. Her *BattleTech* tie-in novel, *The Nellus Academy Incident*, won a Scribe Award. Her editing work has netted her an Australian Shadows Award for *Grants Pass*. Jennifer's short form work has appeared in *Apex Publications*, and in anthologies set in the worlds of *Valdemar*, *Shadowrun*, *V-Wars*, and *Predator*. Jennifer is also the Creative Director of Apocalypse Ink Productions, and was the managing editor of Evil Girlfriend Media and assistant editor for Apex Book Company.

Jennifer has been a freelance author, editor, tie-in writer for over ten years after leaving her high paying tech job, and she's never been happier. She keeps a tight schedule on her writing and editing projects and somehow manages to find time to volunteer for several professional writing organizations such as SFWA, HWA, and IAMTW. She shares her husband, Jeff, with several cats and often uses him as a sounding board for her story ideas.

Visit Jennifer's worlds at jenniferbrozek.com
FaceBook: https://www.facebook.com/jennifer.brozek
Twitter: @JenniferBrozek

About the Illustrator

Elizabeth Guizzetti is the author and illustrator of several independent comics: *Faminelands*, *Lure*, and *Out for Souls & Cookies*. She also creates spot illustrations, maps, and character sketches for authors and gamers. Elizabeth has even been known to write a Science Fiction and Fantasy novel or four. Her debut novel, *Other Systems*, was a 2015 Finalist for the Canopus Award for Excellence in Interstellar Fiction. Her short work has appeared in anthologies such as *Wee Folk and The Wise* and *Beyond the Hedge*.

Elizabeth currently lives in Seattle with her husband and two dogs. When not writing or illustrating, she loves hiking and birdwatching.

Learn more about Elizabeth's work at elizabethguizzetti.com.
Facebook: https://www.facebook.com/Elizabeth.Guizzetti.Author
Twitter: E_Guizzetti

ARTEMIS V
THE ONLY PLANET IN THE EMPIRE WHERE PURPURAN GROWS
A PLANET UNDER SIEGE
A PLANET OF SLAVERY
A PLANET OF MISSING CHILDREN...

THE PRINCE OF ARTEMIS V

WRITTEN BY
JENNIFER BROZEK

Artwork By
ELIZABETH GUIZZETTI

APOCALYPSE INK
PRODUCTIONS

COPYRIGHT © 2018 BY JENNIFER BROZEK & ELIZABETH GUIZZETTI

Apocalypse Ink Productions
6830 NE Bothell Way, STE C #404
Kenmore, WA 98028
Website: http://www.apocalypse-ink.com/
FaceBook: https://www.facebook.com/apocalypseinkproductions/
Twitter: @ApocalypseInk

ISBN: 978-1-940444-34-5

I ENVY HER AND HER IMAGINATION.
I NEVER HAD HER ARTISTIC TALENT. AND I HAVEN'T DRAWN SINCE THAT NIGHT FIVE YEARS AGO.
SINCE TOOR WAS TAKEN...
ON A NIGHT JUST LIKE THIS ONE WHEN THE DOUBLE MOONS OF ARTEMIS V RISE IN THEIR ANNUAL DOUBLE-FULL ARC

SHHHWHUP
THEY ALL LOOK AT ME AS IF SHE'S ALREADY BEEN TAKEN. WE'VE GOT TO DO SOMETHING.
THE COMPANY DOESN'T GIVE A DAMN. AS LONG AS THE FLOWERS ARE HARVESTED AND DYE IS MADE, THEY DON'T CARE.
WE'VE GOT TO DO SOMETHING. ANYTHING. STOP THE PURPURAN SHIPMENTS. GET THEIR ATTENTION...
THE LAST TIME WE TRIED THAT, THE COMPANY ALMOST STARVED US TO DEATH. ALL THEY CARE ABOUT IS THAT DAMN FLOWER.
NOT US. NOT OUR CHILDREN.

THERE ARE NO RESCUERS. NO BRAVE GUARDSMEN. NO HEDARI SLINGING IN TO SAVE THE DAY. WE ONLY HAVE US.
I CAN'T LOSE HER.
WE'RE ON OUR OWN. ALWAYS HAVE BEEN.
THERE ARE NO RESCUERS. NO BRAVE GUARDSMEN. NO HEDARI SLINGING IN TO SAVE THE DAY. WE ONLY HAVE US.

I CAN'T STAND IT.
THEIR PAIN AND HOPELESSNESS...

DESPAIR.

I'LL BLOCK IT OUT.

I DON'T WANT LANTERI TO HEAR IT IN THEIR VOICES.
SHHWHUP

ALL HOPES ARE DASHED ON ARTEMIS V...
IN MY WORLD...

...THIS ONE WAS,
TOO.

...THERE ARE NO TAKERS
AND NO ONE'S AFRAID OF
LOSING THEIR CHILDREN.

I'M GOING TO NORI'S.
WAIT!

WHAT?
UH, DON'T FORGET YOUR COAT.
I'M JUST GOING NEXT DOOR, MOM.
GET YOUR COAT OR YOU'RE NOT GOING ANYWHERE!

BE BACK BEFORE DARK, YOU HEAR ME?
IT'S NOT LIKE IT'S GOING TO GET ALL THAT DARK WITH THE DOUBLE FULL MOON

The Empire thrives
due to Workers;
Workers thrive in The Empire
LANTERI...!
YES, MA'AM. BEFORE DARK. CAN I GO NOW?
YES. GO.
ALL NATURAL
HEDARI PROTEIN PUFFS
SOY PACK

YOU LOOK AT HER AS IF SHE'S ALREADY BEEN TAKEN.
The Empire
due to Workers;
Workers thrive in The Empire
SOY PACK
ALL NATURAL

YOU DON'T KNOW WHAT IT'S LIKE.

I LOST TOOR, TOO!
HE WAS MY TWIN. HE WAS CLOSER TO ME THAN YOU.
YOU ACT LIKE... LIKE... YOU'RE THE ONLY ONE WHO LOST HIM.
DON'T YOU DARE!

NO! DON'T YOU DARE!
CRASH
SCHREECH
ALL NATURAL
HEDARI PROTEIN PUFFS
WE ALL LOST HIM WHEN HE WAS TAKEN
NOW YOU ACT LIKE LANTERI'S ALREADY GONE!

SOB
SOB
Help Captain Puff protect the Purpuran Fields!
TOOR... WAS SPECIAL.
HE WAS YOUR FAVORITE.
HE PROMISED ME HE'D NEVER BE TAKEN. HE PROMISED.
Help Captain Puff protect the Purpuran Fields!
START
END
NOW, LANTERI'S YOUR FAVORITE.
SHE'S THE ONLY GIRL OF AGE IN THIS HARVEST ZONE. SHE'S SPECIAL.
WHAT ABOUT NORI?
SHE'S TOO OLD. THEY HAVEN'T TAKEN ANYONE THAT OLD IN AGES.

WHY AREN'T YOU WORRIED ABOUT ME?
OF COURSE I'M WORRIED ABOUT YOU! WHAT WOULD MAKE YOU THINK...? WHY? OH, HART, I LOVE YOU. I'M WORRIED YOU'LL BE TAKEN.
BUT YOU'RE DIFFERENT. YOU'RE STRONGER. SOLID. DEPENDABLE.
NOT THE PRIZE TOOR WAS AND LANTERI IS?
KE.S BEST OATS
SO
ALL NATURAL
HEDARI PROTEIN PUFFS
I LOVE YOU, HART. YOU'RE THE ONE I CAN DEPEND ON. YOU ALWAYS HAVE BEEN.
THAT'S WHY I NEED YOU TO PROTECT YOUR SISTER.
DON'T WORRY, MOM. I'LL PROTECT HER. I PROMISE.

HEY
WHAT WAS TOOR LIKE?
OF COURSE SHE'D ASK ABOUT HIM TONIGHT.

HE WAS A LOT LIKE YOU. GOOD WITH ANIMALS. A DREAMER. ALWAYS FORGETTING ABOUT THE TIME.
I WAS ALWAYS SAVING HIM FROM PUNISHMENT. REMINDING HIM TO DO HIS CHORES. TO COME HOME ON TIME. ANYTHING MOM AND DAD SAID TO DO.
I'M NOT LIKE THAT. I REMEMBER THINGS.
YOU'RE RIGHT. I GUESS YOU'VE GOT A BIT OF BOTH ME AND TOOR IN YOU. PART DREAMER. PART... NOT DREAMER.
I'M A PRINCESS.

WHAT'S THE FIRST RULE OF BEING A PRINCESS?
NEVER, EVER ABANDON YOUR PEOPLE FOR THEY NEED YOU MORE THAN YOU KNOW.

AND THE SECOND?
A PRINCESS IS A SERVANT TO ALL OF HER PEOPLE.
SHE'S SUPPOSED TO CARE FOR THEM AND NEVER LET THEM DOWN. EVER.

YEP. AND THE THIRD?
A PRINCESS MUST BE KIND AND GENEROUS BUT FIRM BECAUSE SHE HAS TO MAKE HARD DECISIONS THAT OTHERS CANNOT.

YES, BECAUSE NOTHING GOOD EVER COMES EASY.
I KNOW HOW WE'RE GOING TO DEFEAT THE TAKERS.

WHAT? HOW?

YOU'RE GONNA SLEEP IN HERE WITH ME.

IF THEY COME TO TAKE EITHER OF US, THIS WILL CONNECT US AND THE PULLING SHOULD WAKE ONE OF US UP.

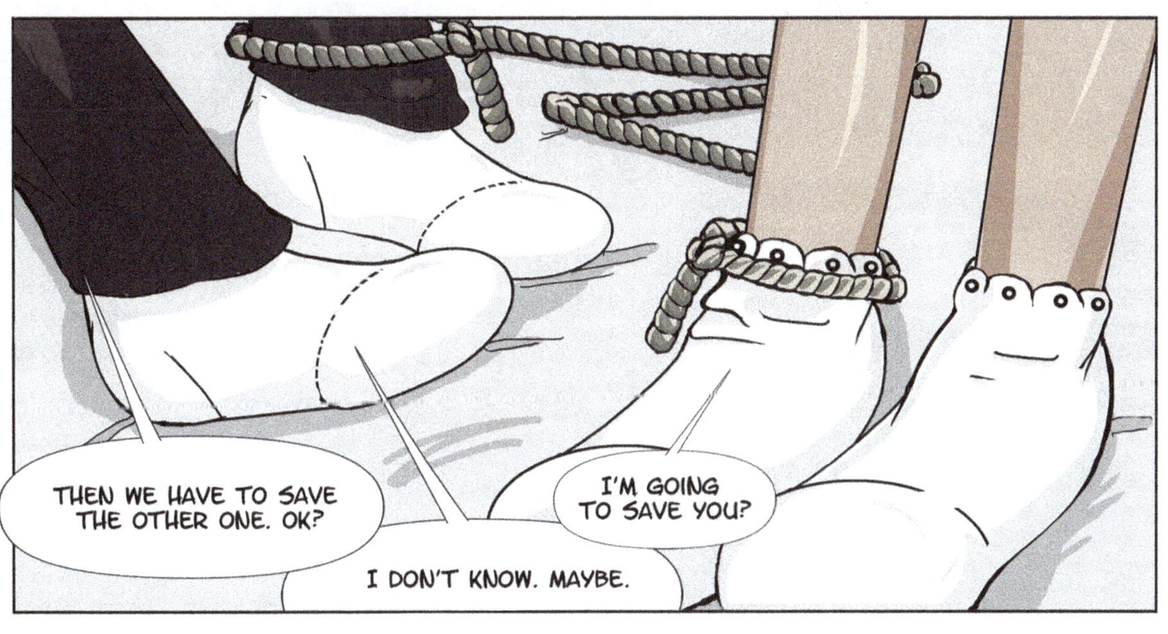

THEN WE HAVE TO SAVE THE OTHER ONE. OK?
I'M GOING TO SAVE YOU?
I DON'T KNOW. MAYBE.

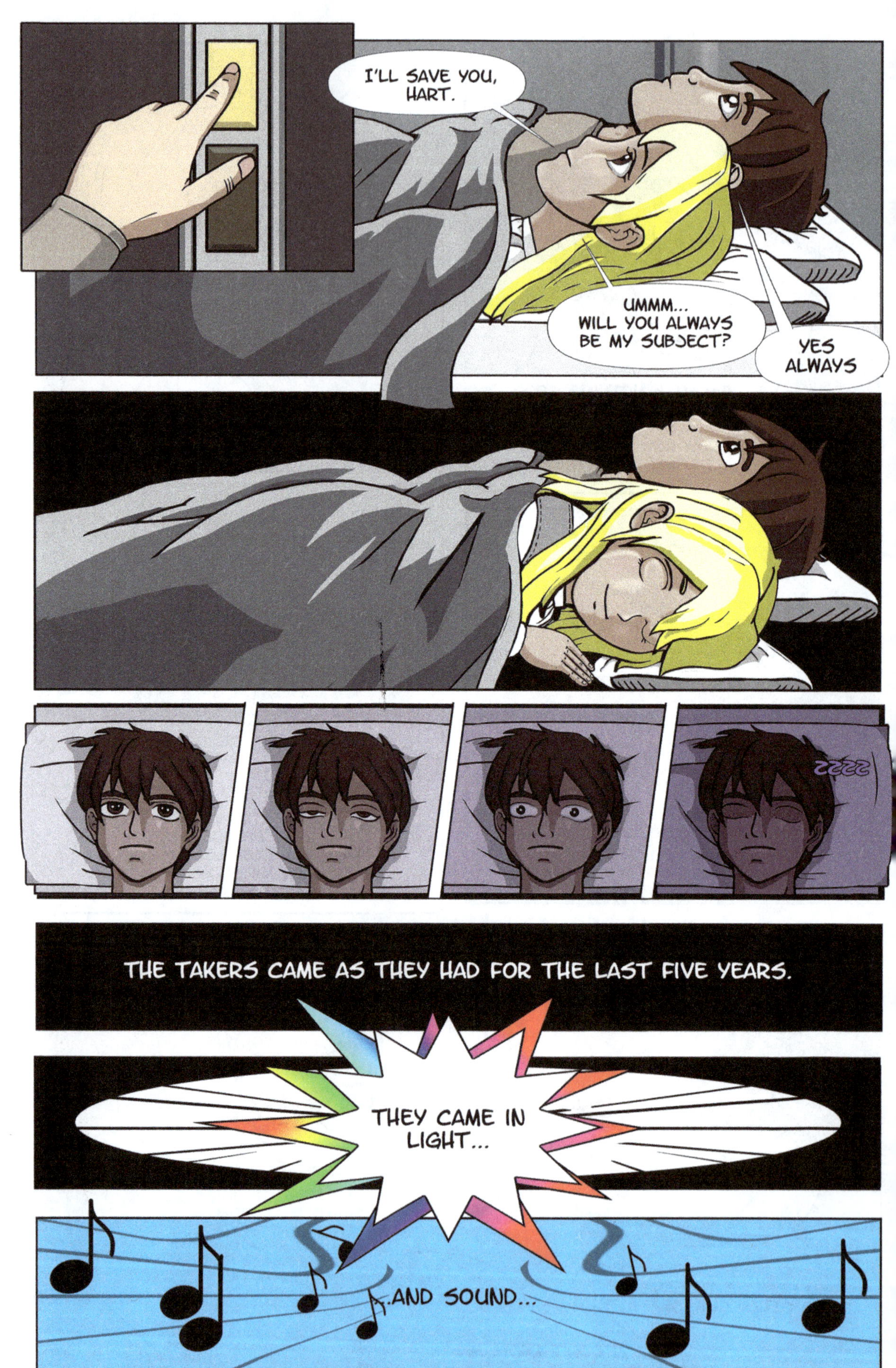

I'LL SAVE YOU, HART.
UMMM... WILL YOU ALWAYS BE MY SUBJECT?
YES ALWAYS
THE TAKERS CAME AS THEY HAD FOR THE LAST FIVE YEARS.
THEY CAME IN LIGHT...
...AND SOUND...

...AND BEAUTY.

WE'RE STILL WAITING FOR YOU.
I CAN'T GO WITH YOU, DAVIN. I CAN'T.

WHY NOT? YOU DESERVE A BETTER LIFE. YOU DESERVE TO PLAY IN THE SUN.
THAT WORLD IS NO PLACE FOR A CHILD.

YOU AREN'T REAL.
YOU CAN'T PROVE YOU'RE REAL AND THAT WHAT YOU SAY ISN'T A LIE.

YOUR BROTHER —

IS DEAD!

NO. FAR FROM IT. HE'S HERE WITH US AND HAPPY. HE MISSES YOU.
HE TOLD ME TO TELL YOU TO REMEMBER THE DAY OF PURPLE HANDS. I DON'T KNOW WHAT THAT MEANS AND HE WOULDN'T TELL ME.

THE DAY OF PURPLE HANDS
WAS THE DAY HE AND TOOR HAD DECIDED THAT IF THEY WERE NOT
ALLOWED TO WEAR THE ROYAL PURPURAN COLOR,
THEY WOULD DYE THEIR SKIN WITH IT.
BOYS!
SANERI, GET YOUR BOYS!
IT HAD BEEN TOOR'S IDEA;
A SMALL ACT OF DEFIANCE AGAINST THE COMPANY AND THE CIRCUMSTANCES
THAT HAD MADE THEIR FAMILY ALL BUT INDENTURED SERVANTS.
THEY HAD BEEN GROUNDED FOR WEEKS.
BUT BOTH OF THEM CONSIDERED IT A VICTORY OVER THE EMPIRE.
IT WAS SOMETHING TOOR WOULD REMIND HIM OF.

IT DOESN'T MATTER.

BUT, WHY? WHY CAN'T YOU COME WITH US?
BECAUSE A PRINCE NEVER ABANDONS HIS PEOPLE — FOR THEY NEED HIM MORE THAN HE KNOWS.

MY TIME IS RUNNING OUT.
I WON'T BE ABLE TO KEEP COMING BACK.
YOU'RE MY OTHER HALF.
THE ONE I WAS MEANT TO SAVE.
IF I CAN'T SAVE YOU,
I DON'T KNOW WHAT I'LL DO.
IT MIGHT KILL ME. PLEASE.
MY SISTER NEEDS ME.

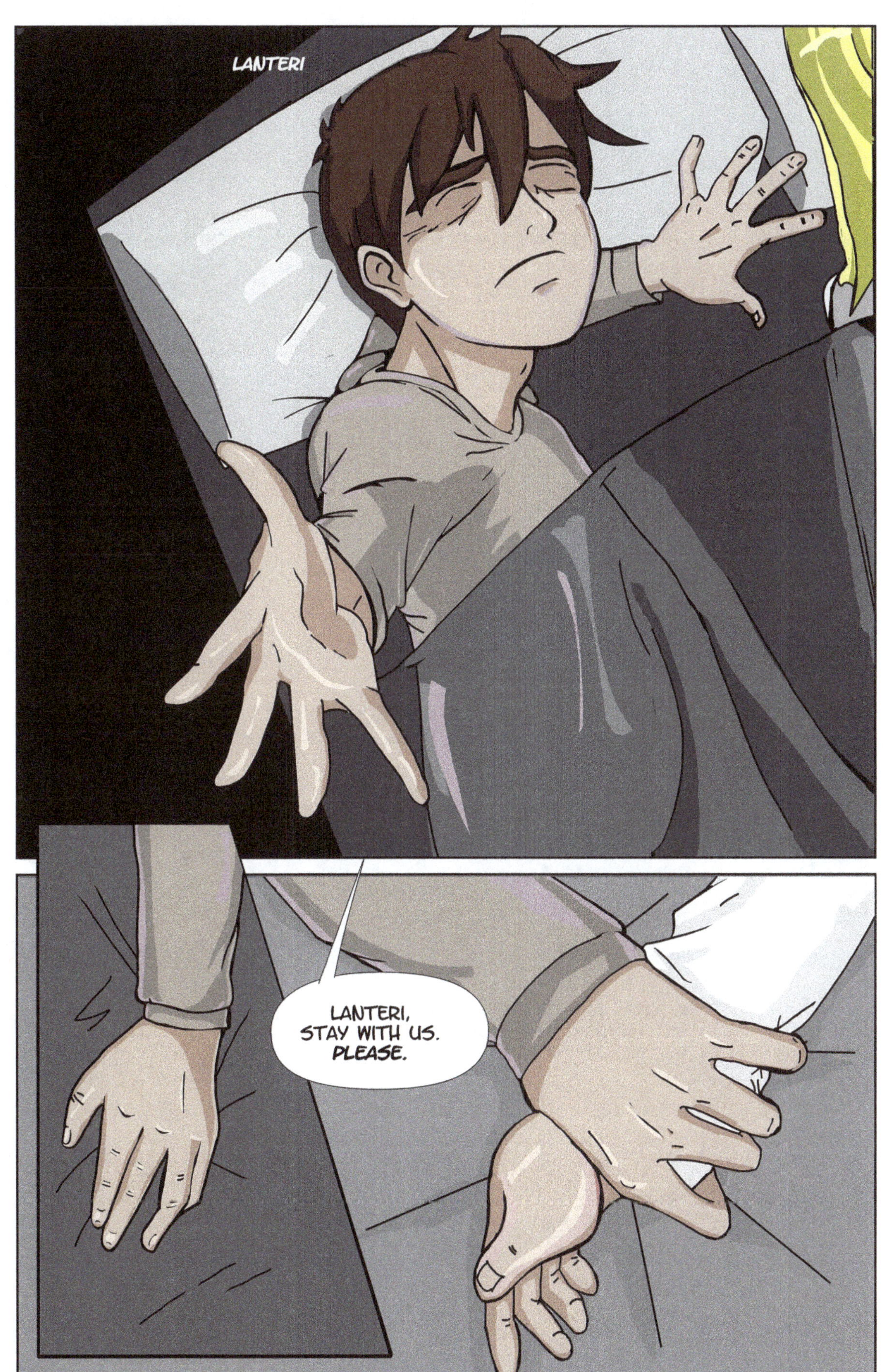

LANTERI
LANTERI, STAY WITH US. PLEASE.

I CAN'T GO WITH YOU.
MY FAMILY NEEDS ME.
AND I CAN'T LET YOU TAKE
LANTERI.

I'LL GO NOW,
BUT I CAN'T WAIT
MUCH LONGER.

WE'LL MEET ONLY ONE MORE TIME,
ON THE NEXT DOUBLE FULL MOON.

YOU HAVE ONE LAST CHANCE TO
FREE YOURSELF OF THAT
HELLISH PLACE.

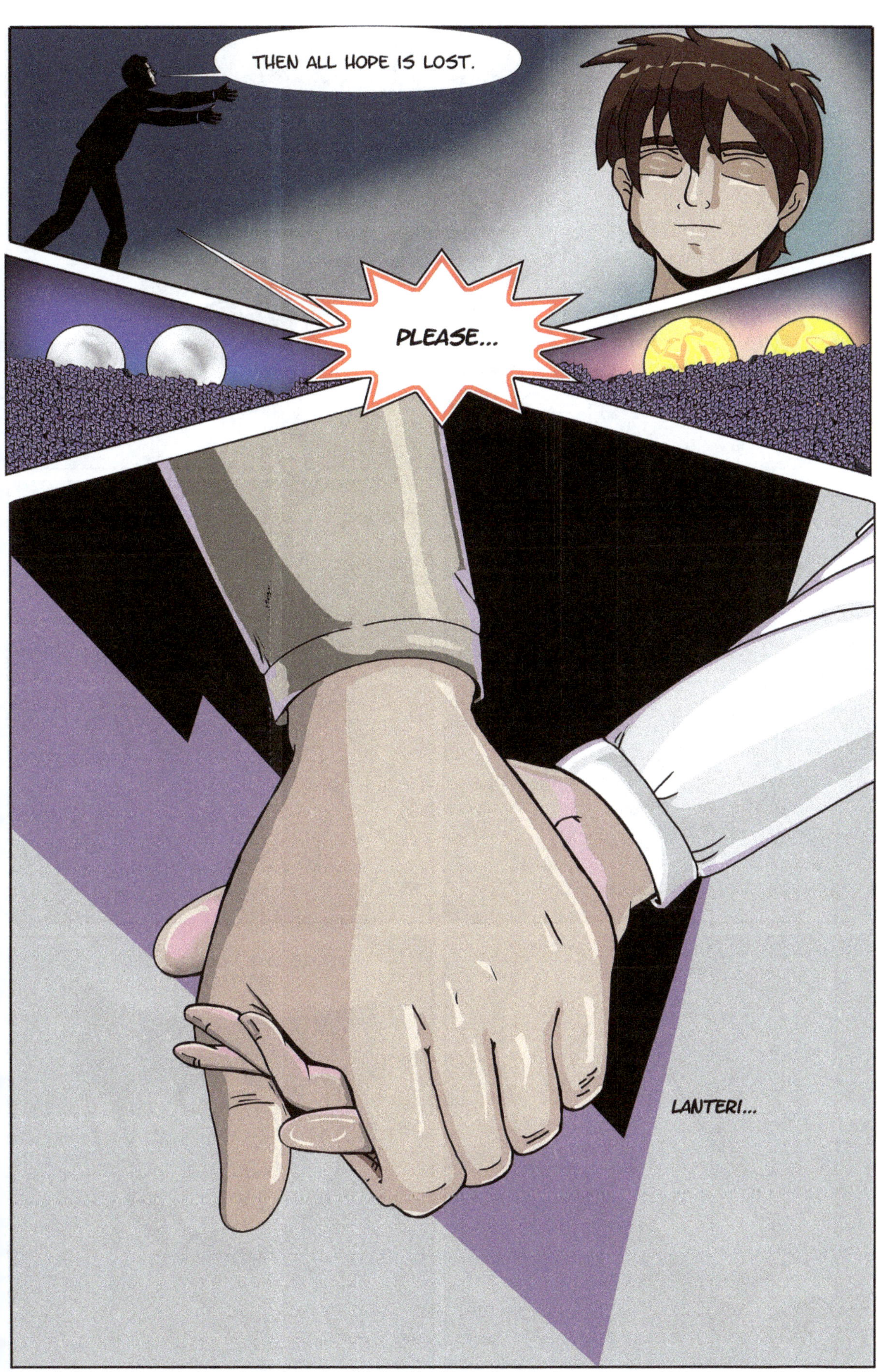

THEN ALL HOPE IS LOST.
PLEASE...
LANTERI...

YOU BRUISED MY ARM.
I'M SORRY.
SNIFF
LOOKS LIKE YOU BRUISED ME TOO.

WHY DIDN'T ANYONE TELL ME THEY'D BE PRETTY...
SHHH, IT'S OK.
YOU WON'T REMEMBER SOON.
YOU WON'T REMEMBER ANYTHING ABOUT IT.
IT'LL BE JUST A DREAM.
NO ONE REMEMBERS, REALLY.
THAT'S WHY NO ONE TALKS ABOUT IT.
THEY WERE SO PRETTY.
JUST LIKE MY DREAM,
MY PICTURE.

I KNOW, LAN, I KNOW.

DO THEY COME FOR YOU EVERY YEAR? IS IT LIKE THAT EVERY YEAR?

HOW DO YOU NOT GO? WHY DO YOU STAY?

I THINK OF YOU. I STAY FOR YOU. YOU NEED ME. AND SO DO MOM AND DAD.

BUT, WHAT IF IT'S NOT A LIE? WHAT IF... IT'S REALLY WHAT THEY SAY?
YOU CAN'T THINK LIKE THAT. YOU CAN'T, LANTERI.
THINK WHAT IT WOULD DO TO MOM AND DAD IF YOU WERE TAKEN. IF WE WERE TAKEN. IT WOULD KILL THEM.

DON'T THINK LIKE THAT EVER.
I CAN'T REMEMBER WHAT SHE LOOKED LIKE. I CAN'T REMEMBER ANYTHING...
I CAN'T REMEMBER ANYTHING BUT THE SHINING SUN.

GO WASH YOUR FACE AND WAKE UP MOM AND DAD. THEY'LL BE GLAD TO KNOW YOU'RE STILL HERE.
I WANT TO REMEMBER.
NO, YOU DON'T

LAST NIGHT DAVIN GAVE ME PROOF TOOR WAS STILL ALIVE AND HAPPY.
HE TOLD ME HOW MUCH HE NEEDED ME... AND OUR NEXT MEETING WOULD BE OUR LAST.
FOR FIVE YEARS, I RESISTED FOR LANTERI'S SAKE NOW, I KNOW THE TAKERS WANT US BOTH.
NEXT YEAR, WE COULD BE TAKEN TO THAT PLACE OF WONDER, BE REUNITED WITH TOOR, AND LIVE OUR LIVES IN THE SUN INSTEAD OF SHADOWS AND MUD.
IT WOULD KILL MY PARENTS TO LOSE ALL OF US TO THE TAKERS.
BUT, RIGHT NOW, I'M NOT CERTAIN THAT KNOWLEDGE IS ENOUGH TO KEEP ME HERE NEXT TIME.

THE PRINCE OF
ARTEMIS V
ALL NATURAL
HEDARI
PROTEIN
PUFFS
THE
HEALTH
OF THE
EMPIRE
DEPENDS
ON
THE
HEALTH
OF THE
WORKERS!
EAT
PROTEIN
PUFFS
FOR
THE
EMPIRE

The Prince of Artemis V
Written by Jennifer Brozek

"A PRINCESS IS A SERVANT TO ALL OF HER PEOPLE. SHE'S supposed to care for them and never let them down. Ever," Lanteri said.

Hart nodded at his little sister. "What's the first rule of being a princess?"

"Never, ever abandon your people—for they need you more than you know," she said in a tone so serious that it would have indicated satire if it had not come from an eight-year-old's mouth.

"You're a very good princess."

"I'm trying." She smiled at her older brother. "But sometimes, it's hard."

"I know. As Dad says, 'Nothing good...'"

" '... ever comes easy,'" they both finished together and then grinned.

Lanteri bent over her pixel board and continued to draw her idea of the perfect castle. She drew each line slowly, dragging the pixel pen over the board. Whenever a line was not exactly as she wanted it, she turned the pixel pen over to erase the offending pixels, before going back to her masterpiece. She had been working on this particular picture for weeks.

Hart watched her, envying both her ability to manipulate the pixel board and her imagination. He, himself, had never had her artistic talent and had not drawn anything since that night five years ago... since Toor was Taken. Though only thirteen, Hart felt old. He felt like his parents must feel after a long day in the fields of harvesting the purpuran flower buds. He hoped that Lanteri would never have to feel the way he felt right now. Especially as the double moons of Artemis V readied themselves to rise in their annual double-full arc tonight.

The opening and closing of the front door signaled the arrival of their parents. Neither child moved from their respective places in their shared bedroom. The conversation between their parents, or argument as it seemed to be, echoed through the small Company-provided house.

"They all look at me like she's already been Taken," Hart heard his mother say. He could imagine the distressed flush of his mother's face. "We've got to do something."

"The Company doesn't give a damn what happens to us. As long as the purpuran flowers are harvested and the royal dye is made, they don't care." In his mind's eye, Hart could see his father's drawn face and strength failing in his old man's body.

"We've got to do something. Anything. Stop the purpuran shipments. Get their attention." His mother's voice had softened to the whine of a wounded animal. "I can't go through this again."

"Saneri, the last time we tried something like that the Company almost starved us to death. The only thing that grows on this mudball is the purpuran flower. The Company doesn't care. The empire doesn't care. The empress herself can't know of this and even if she did, would she care? No. I don't think so. There are no rescuers. No brave guardsmen. No heroic Hedari. No stranger SLINGing in from another galaxy who'll come roaring to the rescue. We only have us to depend on. That's how it's always been."

"I can't go through this again. I can't lose her."

Hart reached over and closed the bedroom door to shut out their parents' pain and worry, and most of all, their helplessness. He hoped Lanteri had not heard their parents' despair but, as all hopes were dashed on Artemis V, this one was too.

"In my world," Lanteri said without looking up from her pixel drawing of a castle in a beautiful sunny landscape, "there are no Takers and no one's afraid of losing their children."

❅

"I'M GOING TO NORI'S," LANTERI CALLED AS SHE HEADED OUT the door.

"Wait!" Saneri called.

Hart, sitting at the kitchen table, heard the panic in his mother's voice and hoped Lanteri would not. He also hoped that their mother would not ground Lanteri on what might be her last day alive.

Lanteri stopped, turned and gave her mother an impatient look. "What?"

"Uh, don't forget your coat."

"I'm just going next door, Mom."

"Don't you sass me. Go get your coat or you're not going anywhere."

Lanteri sighed and stomped back to the bedroom to get her coat. Hart listened as their mother paced, then fussed with Lanteri's coat. "You be back before dark. You hear me?"

"It's not like it's gonna get all that dark with the double full moon, Mom."

Hart smiled at the defiance in his little sister's voice.

"Lanteri…" Their mother's voice had a warning note in it that promised pain and punishment if she were not obeyed.

Another sigh. "Yes, ma'am. Before dark. Can I go now?" Lanteri asked.

There was a pause before their mother's reluctant answer came, "Yes. Ok. Go."

Hart knew their mother would not make that kind of fuss about him if he wanted to go over to a friend's house today. It made him hurt a little more inside. He waited for his mother to come to the kitchen.

Saneri was wiping at her face when she entered. Seeing her son there surprised her. "Hart? What's wrong?"

"You look at her as if she's already been Taken." His voice was flat and full of anger.

Saneri blinked at her eldest in shock and realization. Shock turned to anger in a tightening of her lips. "You don't know what it's like."

"I lost Toor, too. He was my brother. My twin. He was closer to me than you. You act like… like… you're the only one who lost him."

The tightened lips turned into a white line while bright splotches of red shone on Saneri's cheeks. "Don't you dare!"

"No, don't you dare!" Hart stood up, his chair falling away from him to clatter on the floor. "We all lost him when he was Taken. Now, you act like Lanteri's already gone."

Hart's outrage deflated his mother's anger and she slumped to the kitchen chair in front of her like a spent windsock. She put her face in her hands and silently wept into them, her body shaking with her repressed sobs.

It was Hart's turn to be deflated. He watched his mother break down in front of him for a couple of silent moments before picking up the kitchen chair, setting it right and sitting across from her. He let the worst of her grief, anguish and rage pass before offering her a kitchen towel as an apology. For several long minutes, the two of them sat there in silence. Him watching her and her wiping at her face, regaining her composure bit by bit.

"Toor," she said, "was special to me. He promised me he'd never be Taken. He promised me…"

"He was your favorite." There was no accusation in Hart's voice; just a simple knowing truth. Saneri looked away but did not deny it. This lack of denial murdered the last bit of his child's heart. He swallowed his own grief and pressed on. "Now, Lanteri's your favorite."

"She's the only girl child of age in this harvest zone. She's special."

"What about Nori?"

"Nori's too old. They haven't Taken anyone over the age of fifteen in at least twenty years."

"Then why aren't you worried about me?" The betraying words were out of Hart's mouth before he knew he was going to ask the question. But now that the words were on the table between them, he could not snatch them back. At least his mother had the decency to look shocked again.

"What? Of course I'm worried about you! What would make you think…? Why? Oh, Hart, I love you. Of course I'm worried you'll be Taken." She paused, waiting for him to respond but he just continued to look at her, stone-faced. "You're different. You're stronger. Solid. Dependable," she tried to explain.

"Not the prize that Toor was and Lanteri is?"

His mother gave him a look. "Now you're just being sullen. Stop it." She wiped at her face again but this time it was more of a nervous tic.

This casual maternal admonishment made him smile though he did not really understand why. Perhaps it was that the admonishment was a sign that she really did care about him and what he did.

Saneri took the small smile as a sign of encouragement. "I love you, Hart. You're the one I can depend on. You always have been." She paused, took a breath and then forged onward, "That's why I need you to protect your sister."

"Because you and Dad can't."

She looked away and nodded, but not before he saw the flinch of pain on her face. "Yes. You're closer to her. She idolizes you. You… I-I think you're her only hope."

Now that the truth was out between them—almost all of it anyway, Hart nodded at her, feeling better. He was Lanteri's only hope. He knew it. He had always known it. "Don't worry, Mom. I'll protect her. I promise." The look of gratitude on his mother's face was painful but he smiled at it. "I know what to do."

❆

LANTERI AND HART SAT IN THEIR BEDROOM NOT SPEAKING. They both watched the window as the sun set late in the summer's evening. Their silence spoke volumes to each other in sibling-speak. They were both worried. She looked to him for comfort and he gave it in a sudden slap at the button that closed the blinds and signaled the room's automatic sensors to produce a dim light. Then, he patted the spot next to him on his bed nearest the wall. She came willingly enough despite wanting to seem adult. There was enough of a child's need for comfort that she took it went it was offered.

They sat like that on his bed, Lanteri pressed to her brother's side and he with his arm wrapped around her shoulders in a protective embrace. When she spoke, her voice was soft. "What was Toor like?" She could not see Hart's frown but she sensed it and looked up.

He did not look down at her. "He was a lot like you. Good with animals. A dreamer. Always forgetting about the time." Hart smiled, "I was always saving him from punishment. Reminding him to do his chores. To come home on time. To remember what Mom and Dad said to do."

"I'm not like that. I remember things."

Hart looked down at her. "You're right. I guess you've got a bit of both me and Toor in you. Part dreamer. Part... not dreamer."

Lanteri smiled a brave smile at him, "I'm a princess."

"Yes. You are." He returned the smile in kind.

The two of them lapsed into silence again, watching the minutes tick over on the clock. Hart did not know what she thought of but his mind raced. Finally, he shifted, waking Lanteri from her doze.

"What's going on? Are they here?" There was a hint of panic in Lanteri's voice.

"No, silly. We've just got to get ready."

"Oh," she yawned. "How?"

"Like this." Hart reached up to the shelf above his bed and found a small wad of dingy rope. "You're gonna sleep in your clothes tonight and on my bed with me." He tied one end of the rope around his left ankle and then tied the other end of it around her right ankle. "If they come to Take either of us, this will connect us and the pulling should wake one of us up. Then, we have to save the other one. OK?"

"I'm gonna save you?"

He shrugged. "Maybe. I don't know." He kept his head down so she would not see the look on his face. He did not want her to know that he knew what was coming.

Lanteri nodded. "I'll save you." She curled up next to him, facing the wall while he remained on his back.

"Lan?"

"Yeah?"

"What's the first rule of being a princess?"

"Never, ever abandon your people—for they need you more than you know," she said. There was a smile in her sleepy voice.

"Good. And the second?"

Lanteri's body relaxed in the comfort of the familiar game. "A princess is a servant to all of her people. She's supposed to care for them and never let them down. Ever."

"Yep. What's the third rule?"

"A princess must be kind and generous but firm because she has to make the hard decisions that others cannot."

"Because 'nothing good ever comes easy.'" He quoted to her.

There was a moment of silence before she spoke again. "Will you always be my subject?"

"Yes. Always," Hart said. He smiled to himself, allowing his eyes to close and await that which was to come.

❋

THEY CAME AS THEY HAD FOR THE LAST FIVE YEARS. THIS was the sixth time that Hart would face them, the Takers. They came in light, sound and beauty. They looked like they could be any one of a dozen humanoid races but not. They were all beautiful. Shining. Perfect. Too perfect. But, God, they were beautiful. Hart was standing in a field of grass and flowers that could never exist on Artemis V. The sun was shining in that bright, cheerful way that made the Harvesters rush to cover the delicate purpuran flowers that could only survive in the shade.

The air smelled cool, clear and clean. There was no hint of the musty smell the permeated everything on Artemis V. He knew he was still at home in bed, but at the same time, he was also here, in this impossibly perfect place of beauty and light. There were several of them in the distance, the Takers, watching him. He wanted to go to them but refused to be moved. They had to come to him.

A boy approached. It was the same boy who had approached him every year for the last five years. This boy, with brown hair and blue eyes, grew a year older with each meeting so that he and Hart were always peers. Never one older or younger. "Hart, we're still waiting. Waiting for you."

Hart ached at the sound of his name. "I can't go with you." He saw the boy's smile falter and it hurt his soul.

"Please. Hart, why not? You deserve a better life. You deserve to play in the sun and the grass. That world is no place for a child."

Hart shook his head, "You aren't real. You can't prove you're real and that what you say isn't a lie."

The boy sighed with weariness of the familiar argument. He tried something new, "Your brother—"

"Is dead!" Hart interrupted, not willing to listen to anything about Toor. "You killed him five years ago."

The boy shook his head. "No. Far from it. He's here with us and happy. He misses you. He told me to tell you to remember the Day of Purple Hands." For once, the boy did not look happy or sad. He looked confused. "I don't know what that means and he wouldn't tell me."

Hart felt his stomach lurch. The Day of Purple Hands was the day he and Toor had decided that if they were not allowed to wear the royal purpuran purple color, they would dye their skin with it. It had been Toor's idea; a small act of defiance against the Company and the circumstances that had made their family all but indentured servants to those that employed them. They had gotten in so much trouble. They had been grounded for weeks. But both of them had considered it a victory over the Company. It was something Toor *would* remind him of.

But he could not leave Lanteri.

"It doesn't matter." Hart turned from the boy, though it was hard to turn from that light.

"But, why?" There was a desperate plea in the boy's voice. "Why can't you come with us?"

Hart's answer was a whisper. "Because a prince never abandons his people—for they need him more than he knows."

The boy walked up close behind Hart, putting his hand on Hart's shoulder. "My time is running out. I won't be able to keep coming back. You're my other half. You're the one I was meant to save. If I can't save you, I don't know what I'll do. It might kill me. Please."

The feel of the boy's hand on Hart's shoulder was warm and comforting. It almost unraveled his resolve right then and there. The idea that this boy needed him and needed to save him was almost too much. Then, another sensation distracted Hart from the warmth of the boy's hand. Something was tugging at his ankle. He looked down and saw the dingy rope from his shelf that he had tied around his ankle pulled tight. It was not a part of this world. It was a part of his home.

Lanteri.

Lanteri was being Taken. From him, from his mother, from his family. Hart shrugged the boy's hand from his shoulder. "My sister needs me." He closed his eyes and groped for his sister. At first, he thought he was too late, and then his hand found his sister curled in a tight ball in the corner of the bed. He grabbed her upper arm and squeezed tight. "Lanteri, stay with us," he whispered to her, praying she could hear him.

Hart opened his eyes upon that field of beauty and light, drinking in the wonder that it was. In his hand, he could feel, but not see, Lanteri's arm. "I can't go with you. My family needs me. And I can't let you take Lanteri." He felt the boy step back from him but did not turn around. He could not turn around to see the sorrow he knew was etched all over the boy's perfect face. It would be too much to bear.

"I'll go now," the boy said. "But I can't wait much longer. We'll meet only one more time on the next double full moon. You have one last chance to free yourself of that hellish place and then, all hope is lost. Please…"

Hart squinched his eyes shut against the temptation of this place and willed that the boy with his promises of light and joy would just go away. Mercifully, the scent of that place disappeared and the boy did not speak again.

❄

"YOU BRUISED MY ARM," LANTERI SAID AS SHE LOOKED AT the finger shaped marks on her arm in the twilight of the morning. Her voice was subdue as she refused to look at him.

"I'm sorry," Hart said, apologizing for more than the bruise, as he bent over to untie the rope from around their ankles. As he wadded up the rope again, he could have sworn he smelled that other world on it. He threw it from him towards the shelf and did not bother to see if he hit his mark. He looked down and saw a bruise around his ankle. "You bruised me, too."

Lanteri turned in a sudden motion, threw her arms around him and pressed her face into his chest. Her voice came out in choked sobs. "Why didn't you tell me it'd be like that? Why didn't anyone tell me they'd be so pretty?"

He hugged her to him and petted her hair. "Shhhh," he said as he rocked her. "Shhh, it's OK. You won't remember soon. You won't remember anything about it. It'll be just a dream. No one remembers, really. That's why no one talks about it."

"They were so pretty. It was just like my dream, my picture."

"I know, Lan, I know."

She pulled away from him and looked at his face, "Do they come for you every year? Is it like that every year?"

He smoothed away a tear smudge from her cheek and nodded, not wanting to lie to her again. He grimaced at the look of pain on her face.

"How do you not go? Why do you stay?"

Hart closed his eyes and wondered that himself. "I think of you," he said. "I stay because of you. You need me. And so do mom and dad."

"But, what if it's not a lie? What if... it's really what they say?"

"You can't think like that. You can't, Lanteri. Think of what it would do to mom and dad if you were Taken. If we were Taken. It would kill them." Hart shook his head. "Don't think like that ever." He could hear the lack of conviction in his voice and was certain that she could, too.

She frowned, "I can't remember what she looked like. I can't remember anything but the shining sun."

He turned from her, "Go wash your face and then wake up mom and dad. They'll be glad to know you're still here."

Lanteri got up and walked to the door. She paused, looking back at him, "I want to remember." When he did not answer, she shook her head and left to do as he told her to do.

He shook his own head, murmuring "No, you don't," under his breath. He did not remember most of the time. It was only in the weeks before the next double full moon that he would remember the field with the flowers and the boy. Last night was the first time the boy had given him proof that Toor was still alive and happy. Last night was the first time the boy had told him how much he needed Hart and that their next meeting would be their last.

For five years, Hart had resisted for the sake of Lanteri, if not for his parents. Now, he knew for certain the Takers wanted both him and his little sister. Next year, they both could be Taken to that place of wonder, to be reunited with Toor, and to live their lives in the sun instead of the shadows and mud. He knew it would kill their parents to lose all of their children to the Takers but, right now, Hart was not certain that knowledge would be enough next time.

The End

ARTEMIS V
SAFEST PLANET IN THE EMPIRE!

•LIFELONG CAREER OPPORTUNITIES•
•MODERN FAMILY HOUSING•
•EDUCATION FOR EVERY CHILD•
•HEDARI TESTING AVAILABLE•